FiZZY T.V. STAR

Michael Coleman

Illustrated by
Philippe Dupasquier

ORCHARD BOOKS

ORCHARD BOOKS
96 Leonard Street, London EC2A 4RH
Orchard Books Australia
14 Mars Road, Lane Cove, NSW 2066
ISBN 1 85213 996 X (hardback)
ISBN 1 86039 234 2 (paperback)
First published in Great Britain 1995
First paperback publication 1996
Text © Michael Coleman 1995
Illustrations © Philippe Dupasquier 1995
The right of Michael Coleman to be identified as the author
and Philippe Dupasquier as the illustrator of this work has been
asserted by them in accordance with the
Copyright, Designs and Patents Act, 1988.
A CIP catalogue record for this book
is available from the British Library.
Printed in Great Britain by Guernsey Press, C.I.

CONTENTS

1

Rather a Mess

"Do you know you've got a dirty smudge on your knee?" asked Maya, as she and Fizzy practised juggling in the playground before school.

Fizzy looked down. As usual, her best friend was right.

"Oh, no!" she said. "It must be grease. The chain came off my bike on the way to school this morning."

She bent down and rubbed her knee with her handkerchief.

"Now you've got an even *bigger* smudge on your knee," said Maya. "And your hands are greasy, too."

Fizzy looked at her hands. Maya was right again.

This time she gave her dirty knee a really hard rub with her handkerchief, gave her other knee a rub for good luck, and then rubbed both her hands. Finally she blew her nose.

"Now you've got a big smudge on your nose!" cried Maya. "You've got smudges everywhere!"

Fizzy looked at her handkerchief.

"Oh, no! I remember now. I held the chain with my handkerchief – so that I wouldn't get myself greasy!"

"Well it didn't work," laughed Maya. "I think you'd better get cleaned up before Mrs Grimm sees you."

Fizzy hurried in to the school washroom, still juggling.

Lucy Hardwick was there, making sure the ribbons on her pigtails were in exactly the same place on both sides.

"Did you know you've got two dirty knees, two filthy hands and a horrible smudgy nose?" she asked, adding nastily, "as usual".

"Yes thanks, Lucy," said Fizzy. She bounced one of her juggling balls off Lucy's head for Maya to catch. "And did you know you've got a nut like concrete?"

"Fizzy," said Maya, "you'd better hurry up. I think the bell is about to go."

Maya was right, of course. At that moment, the bell went.

"Oh, no!" said Fizzy for the third time that morning. She looked at herself in the mirror. "I haven't got time to clean myself up now."

"What are you going to do?" asked Maya.

Fizzy grinned. "Keep my head down, Maya. You never know, maybe Mrs Grimm will think I'm working!"

"Now, pay attention!" called Mrs Grimm.

At the back of the class, in her place just behind Lucy Hardwick, Fizzy peeped over the top of her book. This was one day when she did *not* want to be the centre of Mrs Grimm's attention.

11

But, at that moment, Mrs Grimm was too busy being excited to notice anyone else.

"You are all going to be on television!" she said, beaming, as everybody in the class stared at her with their eyes wide open. "On *Millington Today*! They want to film a school class at work, and they have chosen us!"

Everybody cheered loudly. *Millington*

Today was the local news programme on television every night.

"Will Andy Bright be coming?" shouted somebody.

Andy Bright was *Millington Today*'s star presenter.

"No, Andy Bright won't be coming, I'm afraid," said Mrs Grimm. "The television people told me that tomorrow is his day off. But another presenter will be coming, of course, and there'll be cameras and lights, and in the evening you'll all be able to go home and see yourselves on your very own television sets!"

That was when Lucy Hardwick's hand went up.

"Yes, Lucy dear?"

"Does that mean we'll all have to be neat and tidy, Mrs Grimm?" asked Lucy Hardwick, sneaking a look behind her at Fizzy. Fizzy ducked her head right down behind her book.

"You most certainly *will* have to be neat and tidy," said Mrs Grimm.

"Really neat? And really tidy?"

"Definitely," said Mrs Grimm. "We want everybody to see a class to be proud of."

Fizzy sank down lower in her seat.

"So we mustn't have a dirty face or anything like that?" Lucy Hardwick went on.

"Indeed not!" exclaimed Mrs Grimm sternly. "Dirty faces will be forbidden! And dirty hands! And dirty knees for that matter! I don't want to see any dirty bits at all!"

Fizzy sank even lower.

" Or we won't be on the television?" said Lucy Hardwick.

"Quite right, Lucy," said Mrs Grimm. "But why do you ask? You're always so beautifully neat and tidy, dear."

"I wasn't thinking of me," said Lucy Hardwick. "I was thinking of somebody else."

As Lucy turned round to look at her, Fizzy sank down once more. Unfortunately, it was one sink too many. With a sudden clatter she slipped off her chair and pulled it down on top of her.

"Fiona Izzard!" bellowed Mrs Grimm, striding towards the back. "Stop fighting with that chair at once!"

Fizzy stuck out her hand as she tried to get up. But all she managed to do was knock her juggling balls off her desk and on to the floor beneath Mrs Grimm's feet.

Fizzy's teacher stepped on one, then

another, then the third.

"Eeeeeekkkk!!"

As Mrs Grimm slithered across the floor,

the juggling balls came bouncing down on top of her one at a time.

"Fiona Izzard!!" roared Mrs Grimm, struggling to her feet. "Come out at once!"

Fizzy crawled out from beneath her desk. Mrs Grimm didn't look happy. Was there anything she could say that would help?

"Hello, Mrs Grimm. You're ever so good at juggling, aren't you?"

For some reason, that didn't seem to work. If anything, it put Mrs Grimm in an even worse mood, so that when she finally caught sight of Fizzy's dirty face, dirty hands and dirty knees she let out her loudest screech yet.

"Fiona Izzard!! You look like a mud pie!"

With a wrinkled nose, Mrs Grimm marched Fizzy to the classroom door.

"To the washroom!" she bellowed. "And if you come to school looking like that tomorrow, there will be no television programme for you. You will be turned off!"

2

Sparkler!

Bbbrrrriiiinnnngggggg!!!

As the alarm went off in Fizzy's ear, she shot up in bed.

What was happening? Was it a fire? Was she late for school? Or had she fallen asleep in class and the school was on fire? What?

Then she saw the alarm clock on her bedside table and remembered – her plan. It had seemed a good idea the night before ...

But now, at six o'clock in the morning?...Yes, it was *still* a good plan!

Bleary-eyed, Fizzy crawled out of bed and tottered to the bathroom ...

... where she washed her hair and had a bath and washed her face and had another bath.

"There's going to be nothing messy about me today," she muttered to herself as she went back to her room ...

... where she put on a sparkling pair of socks, a dazzling white blouse, a wonderfully clean skirt, and a sparklingly, dazzlingly, wonderfully, perfectly clean school top before heading downstairs ...

... where she found a large, black bin-liner and, cutting a hole at the top for her to see through, slipped it over her clothes while she had her breakfast.

"There will be nothing messy about me today," muttered Fizzy once more, as she took off the bin-liner, picked up her school bag, left the kitchen ...

... and went out of the back door, down to the bottom of the garden, over to her bicycle – and straight past it!

That was part of Fizzy's plan, too. Today, she was taking no chances. She was leaving her bike behind and going to school on the bus instead.

There would be nothing messy about her today!

"Fizzy?" said Maya as Fizzy arrived at the bus stop. "Is that you?"

"Sure is," said Fizzy, holding her arms out wide and giving a twirl. "As clean as a whistle. Mrs Grimm can't complain about me today, can she?"

"She can if you don't stay like it," said a squeaky voice. It was Lucy Hardwick, at the front of the bus queue.

"Well I *am* going to stay like it," said Fizzy.

"I can't get greasy from a bicycle chain if I haven't got a bicycle with me, can I?"

"No," agreed Maya.

"There you are then," laughed Fizzy. "How else could I get myself messed up?"

Maya looked thoughtful.

"Well," she said helpfully, "you might sit on some chewing gum. The bus seats have had chewing gum on them before now."

"Maya ..." Fizzy began.

"Or you could get squirted with ink if somebody was filling up their pen and the bus went over a bump. That happened once."

"...Maya, I wasn't serious!"

"Oh, yes!" said Maya. "And then there was the time somebody sat in front of a workman just as he took a bite out of one of his tomato sauce sandwiches ..."

"Maya! Stop!"

Fizzy was a bag of nerves. It sounded as if she would have been safer going to school on her bike after all.

"Why don't you come up here with me, Fizzy?" squeaked Lucy Hardwick from the front of the queue.

Fizzy blinked. Lucy Hardwick? Being nice? To her?

"You can get on the bus first and choose the best seat," said Lucy. "That way you'll stay beautifully clean."

"Well ... er ... thanks, Lucy," said Fizzy as she went forward to stand in front of Lucy Hardwick. "Thanks very much."

"You're welcome," smiled Lucy.

And she meant it. Because what Fizzy hadn't noticed was what Lucy Hardwick *had* noticed – a big muddy puddle, right near the kerb, just waiting for something to drive straight through it.

Which something did. A lorry. A very big

lorry.

Sploosh!!

"My top!" yelled Fizzy as a large splodge of muddy water splashed all over her school top.

"Oh dear," said Lucy Hardwick, peeping over Fizzy's shoulder. "Never mind. It'll wash out. Tomorrow," she added with a nasty laugh.

"Tomorrow's no good!" shouted Fizzy. "The *Millington Today* people are coming today! Mrs Grimm will leave me out! What am I going to do?"

Maya had seen what had happened. "Can't you wash it out when you get to school?"

"That'll be too late, Maya. There won't be time to get it dry."

'No,' thought Fizzy, 'this is a problem that

has to be solved here and now.' She looked around ...

"A-ha! That's the answer! There!"

"What? Where?" asked Maya.

But Fizzy was already on the move, taking off her school top as she dashed towards the rainwater barrel she had just seen at the side of a nearby house.

Leaning over the fence, Fizzy turned the tap at the side of the barrel. As the water gushed out she held her school top underneath it and rubbed furiously.

A minute later she was back again, holding her top up for Maya to inspect.

"There you go. One splodge-free zone!"

"Perfect," said Maya. "But ... haven't you forgotten something?"

"What?"

Maya pointed at the large damp patch on the front of Fizzy's top. "You've still got to get it dry before you can wear it."

Just then the bus came round the corner towards them.

"No problem, Maya!" called Fizzy as she went back to her spot at the head of the queue. "Guess who's just had another idea?"

"You?"

"Got it in one!"

"Oh dear," said Maya.

3

A Bit of a Flap

As the bus came to a stop, Fizzy darted up the stairs to the top deck.

"Right," she said, looking around, "where's the best place to sit?"

"The back seat's empty" said Maya, coming up behind her.

"No, the back seat's no good," said Fizzy.

"How about a front seat?" suggested Maya. "One of those is free."

"The front seat's no good either," said Fizzy. "I need – that one!"

She scurried along the aisle to an empty seat on the side. Maya sat down next to her.

"What has this seat got that the others haven't got?" she asked.

Fizzy pointed. Above her head there was a small sliding window. "That!"

"A window?" said Maya. "What do you need a window for?"

Fizzy held up her wet school top. "Maya, I've got a wet top, right?"

"Yes."

"So ..."

Maya had a nasty feeling. Whenever Fizzy said "So ...", trouble was usually close behind.

"So..." said Fizzy, "if I put my top out like this ..." Standing up, she slid the window open and pushed her school top through the gap.

"... but hang onto it like this ..."

Keeping one cuff inside, Fizzy slid the window back to hold it tight.

"... ta-ra! Never heard of hanging out your washing, Maya? You watch – by the time we get to school my top will have been blow-dried!"

The bus started off.

Outside, Fizzy's top flapped slightly.

As the bus picked up speed it flapped a little more. Then more and more until, as the bus hit top speed, Fizzy's top was

flipping and flapping and wiggling and waggling like mad.

"There you go!" yelled Fizzy. "Perfect!"

The bus began to slow down. As it stopped to let more people on board, Fizzy's top fell limp.

"It's not working," said a miserable Lucy Hardwick from the seat behind, *wishing* it wasn't.

"Yes it is, Lucy," said Fizzy. "Look!" She was right. Outside the window, the damp patch on her school top was fading already.

The bus moved off again, quickly getting up to top speed until Fizzy's top was flapping like a flag with two arms.

"It's nearly dry," said Fizzy, as the bus halted once more.

"Only one more stop to go," said Maya. "The next one's ours, remember."

"One more stop is all that's needed, Maya!" Fizzy could see that the damp patch on her top had almost vanished. "Who cares if Andy Bright can't come today," she said excitedly, "Fizzy Bright will be on the screen instead!"

"Ooh!" said Lucy Hardwick suddenly. "Is that Mrs Grimm down there?"

"Where?" said Fizzy, looking down at the people getting on the bus. She didn't fancy having to explain why her school top was hanging around like it was. Maya looked

out too.

But Mrs Grimm wasn't there. She never had been.

Carefully, while Fizzy and Maya weren't looking, Lucy Hardwick stretched up to the window and pushed it back ever so slightly with her ruler.

"I didn't see her," said Fizzy as the bus started off again.

"No?" said Lucy Hardwick. "I must have been seeing things. Silly me."

The bus began to speed up. Flip, flap, went Fizzy's school top.

It swung into the bus driver's favourite stretch of open road alongside the River Millington. Flippety, flappety, went Fizzy's top.

Fizzy was grinning from ear to ear as she watched it. "Brilliant idea, eh?"

And then the bus hit top speed.

Flippety, flappety, flippety, flappety ... thwumpp! With a noise like an exploding bag, Fizzy's top shot away from the window and rocketed up into the air.

"My top!" yelled Fizzy.

"Oh, yes, a brilliant idea!" laughed Lucy Hardwick, as Fizzy scampered down the stairs.

"Stop the bus! I want to get off!" yelled Fizzy, ringing the driver's bell like mad.

High in the air her top was flying off towards the River Millington, its arms still flapping wildly.

"Oh, look," said Lucy Hardwick, nastily. "It's waving goodbye."

4

Fizzy Goes Fishing

Fizzy raced back down the road to the spot where she'd seen her top sail towards the river. She looked around. It was nowhere to be seen.

'Ah!' thought Fizzy, as she noticed a man sitting under a tree on the river bank, fishing. 'Maybe he saw where my top went. I'll go and ask him'.

Carefully, making sure she didn't get the slightest bit muddy, she scurried across towards him.

"Excuse me," said Fizzy. "Did you see a Millington Junior School top come this way?"

But the man, who had a woolly bobble-hat pulled down tightly over his ears to keep him warm, didn't seem to hear. He

just sat there with his back to her, his fishing line dangling in the deep water.

"Excuse me!" repeated Fizzy, raising her voice. "Did you see a school top come this way? It flew over here like a kite!"

This time the man turned round.

"Have I had a bite?" he said. He shook his head, pointing at the large empty basket beside him. "No, I haven't caught a thing!"

"No, no," shouted Fizzy, "I'm looking for my school top!"

"Stop?" said the man. "Oh no. I don't mind. It's a nice way to spend my day off."

"I didn't say stop!" Fizzy couldn't help laughing. "I said top!"

"Hang on," said the man, "I can't hear you

properly with this bobble-hat on."

He rolled the sides of his bobble-hat up above his ears. "There. That's better. Now, what were you saying?"

"My school top," said Fizzy. "Did you see it? It flew over here like a kite!"

Mr Bobble-hat shook his head. "No. Sorry."

Fizzy looked around again. Her top *had* to be somewhere. It may have been flying like a kite, but it couldn't just have vanished into thin air could it?

Or could it? Of course it could – if it was still *in* the air!

Fizzy looked up into the branches of the tree Mr Bobble-hat was sitting under.

"There it is!"

Fizzy's top had landed in the tree and was hanging from a high branch. All she had to

do was go up and get it. But how? It was Mr Bobble-hat who provided the answer.

"Allow me," he smiled.

Winding in his line, he pulled his fishing rod from the water. Then he came over, pushed the rod up into the branches, and hooked Fizzy's top off with its end.

"At least I can say I've caught something today," he laughed as he lowered Fizzy's school top to the ground.

"Thank you!" beamed Fizzy.

She looked at her top. The damp spot had dried completely and it was back to its sparklingly, dazzlingly, wonderfully, perfectly clean best. All she had to do was put it on, dash back to school and get into class before the bell went. Surely nothing could go wrong now?

"*Millington Today*, here I come!" she shouted happily.

"Pardon?" said Mr Bobble-hat, surprised.

"I said ..." began Fizzy. She stopped. Mr Bobble-hat, in turning to look at her, wasn't watching where he was going. And in front of him was his big, empty basket ...

"Look out!" yelled Fizzy.

She was too late. As he took one step further, Mr Bobble-hat tripped over his

basket – and fell headlong into the river!

"Help!" he shouted, waving his arms wildly. "Help! I can't swim!"

Fizzy ran round in circles. What could she do? Mr Bobble-hat was splashing and struggling in the water. She had to do something. But what?

"Er – don't go away!" she shouted.

"Help! Pull me out! Help!"

Fizzy looked about for something to use. Mr Bobble-hat's fishing rod! That would be perfect. Where was it?

Then she saw it. The fishing rod had fallen into the river, too. It was floating away, out of reach.

What else could she use? She looked down at the school top she was still holding in her hands. Her sparklingly, dazzlingly, wonderfully, perfectly clean school top ...

"Help!"

As Mr Bobble-hat shouted again, Fizzy slithered down the side of the bank. Her foot landed in a big blob of mud, which squelched up into her shoe and over her sock. She held out her school top towards Mr Bobble-hat.

"Grab hold!" she shouted.

"I can't reach it!"

There was only one thing to do. Spreading herself full length on the muddy river bank and leaning over, Fizzy threw her top into

the water while she held tightly to one of its
arms.

With a splash and a shout, Mr Bobble-hat
grabbed it and pulled himself to safety.

"Thank you, thank you," he said, as he
climbed out of the water.

But Fizzy wasn't listening. As she
struggled to her feet again, her mind was
on other things. What was she going to do
now?

She was covered from head to toe in mud. If she was going to stand any chance at all of appearing on *Millington Today*, she had to get to school and get cleaned up – fast!

Off she dashed, up towards the road.

"Wait!" shouted Mr Bobble-hat, holding up Fizzy's sopping wet top. "Stop! Come back!"

As she reached the road somebody in a large van shouted "Stop!", too.

But Fizzy wasn't stopping for anything. Away she went, away from Mr Bobble-hat, away from the van, and she didn't stop until she reached the school gates.

5

That's Her!

Maya was there, hopping up and down as she waited for Fizzy.

"Quick!" she said, as Fizzy scooted round the corner. "The bell's gone! Everybody's in class! You're going to be ... going to be ..."

Maya's mouth fell open when she saw the state Fizzy was in.

"I'm going to be in trouble, Maya," said Fizzy, "if I don't get cleaned up fast!"

Through their classroom window she could see Mrs Grimm. She could see the others. But there was no sign of any television people. There was still time!

"You don't need cleaning up," said Maya, "you need a whole new set of clothes."

Fizzy looked down at her dirty socks, muddy skirt and filthy blouse. Maya was right. She did need a whole new set of clothes. Or did she?

"It's all right, Maya. These clothes *are* clean!"

"Clean!" cried Maya. "Fizzy, look at them. They're filthy!"

"But they're clean on the inside," said Fizzy. "I can turn them inside out!"

She looked across at Mrs Grimm, still bustling about in class. "All I've got to do is get across to the washroom without Mrs Grimm seeing me."

"And how are you going to do that?" asked Maya.

"Easy," laughed Fizzy. "Start walking, Maya. I'll be right behind you!"

As Maya walked across the playground, Fizzy crept along behind her. She peeped out. In class Fizzy could see that Lucy Hardwick had her hand up as usual.

All she had to do was get past the classroom window and she'd be safe. Leaving Maya to go on ahead, Fizzy ducked down low and began to creep along under the window. Further, further, nearly there ...

"Fiona Izzard!!" bellowed a familiar voice.

Fizzy looked up – and saw Mrs Grimm, leaning out of the window above her head. What bad luck! After she'd finished listening to Lucy Hardwick she must have come straight over to the window and spotted her.

Fizzy was right. Mrs Grimm had done just that.

For what Lucy Hardwick had been saying to her was, 'Please Mrs Grimm, Fiona Izzard is creeping across the playground behind Maya Sharma and she is all muddy and horrible.'

Fizzy stood where she'd been told to stand – outside the classroom door. Little pools of water formed around her feet.

Inside, she could hear Mrs Grimm making the final preparations before the television people arrived.

"Ready everybody? My, don't you all look nice and tidy? Especially you, Lucy dear. Oh ... here they come!"

Fizzy watched as a large van with *Watch Millington Today!* on its side turned through the school gates and pulled up.

A lady jumped out at once, lifting a camera onto her shoulder. Behind her, a man carried out a bright light. And behind him ...

Fizzy couldn't believe her eyes. Behind him, was Mr Bobble-hat!

"There she is! That's her!"

Mr Bobble-hat had come through the doors. Now he was heading down the corridor with the camera lady and the lights man hurrying behind him. And he was heading towards her, carrying the wet school top and leaving a trail of muddy water behind him!

"Is your name Fiona Izzard?"

"It most certainly is," said Mrs Grimm, who had rushed to the classroom door to find out what was going on. "Why, what *else* has she done?"

"Not a lot of fun?" said Mr Bobble-hat, whose woolly bobble-hat had slipped over his ears again. "You're right, it wasn't."

"No, no," shouted Mrs Grimm, staring at him in horror. "I said what else has she done?"

"Only saved his life, that's all," said the man with the light. He handed Mr Bobble-hat a microphone.

Mr Bobble-hat spoke into it. "River rescue

report for *Millington Today*," he said.

"River rescue?" said Mrs Grimm. "*Millington Today*?"

"Hey, you're supposed to be taking pictures of us," squeaked Lucy Hardwick as the camera lady zoomed in on Fizzy. "Not her!"

"We will be," said the camera lady. "But this comes first. It's going to be the main item in tonight's programme. We saw the rescue as we were on the way. It's all on film! We just need an interview with the heroine first."

She turned to Mr Bobble-hat. "All ready to go."

"You think it's going to snow?"

"No, no!"

"Hang on," said Mr Bobble-hat, "I can't hear you properly. Let me take this hat off."

As he did so, Fizzy's eyes popped out. So did Mrs Grimm's. So did the eyes of everybody else.

"You're Andy Bright!" cried Fizzy.

"They told me it was your day off today," said Mrs Grimm.

"It is," said the television presenter. "And on my day off I like to go fishing." He smiled at Fizzy. "Not drowning!"

As the lights were switched on and the camera started filming, Andy Bright held up Fizzy's soaking school top.

"Today on *Millington Today*," he said to the camera, "Fiona Izzard and how her school top came to the rescue!"

"Hey, Fizzy's the tops!" yelled somebody.

Andy Bright laughed. "Yes, she is! She certainly saved my day!"